For Ruth – P.M.

For Olive – T.N.

LADYBIRD BOOKS

UK | USA | Canada | Ireland | Australia
India | New Zealand | South Africa

Ladybird Books is part of the Penguin Random House group of companies
whose addresses can be found at global.penguinrandomhouse.com.

www.penguin.co.uk   www.puffin.co.uk   www.ladybird.co.uk

 Penguin
Random House
UK

First published 2021
001

Written by Peter Millett
Illustrated by Tony Neal
Text and illustrations copyright © Ladybird Books Ltd, 2021

Printed in China

The authorized representative in the EEA is Penguin Random House Ireland,
Morrison Chambers, 32 Nassau Street, Dublin D02 YH68

A CIP catalogue record for this book is available from the British Library

ISBN: 978–0–241–49361–8

All correspondence to:
Ladybird Books, Penguin Random House Children's
One Embassy Gardens, 8 Viaduct Gardens, London SW11 7BW

MIX
Paper from
responsible sources
FSC
www.fsc.org   FSC® C018179

THE DINOS ON THE BUS

Written by
PETER MILLETT

Illustrated by
TONY NEAL

The dinos on the bus go,
"Roar, roar, roar!
Roar, roar, roar!
Roar, roar, roar!"

The dinos on the bus go,

"Roar,

roar,

roar!"

All through the land.

The teacher on the bus goes,
"Sit down, please!
Sit down, please!"

Sit down, please!

The teacher on the bus goes,

"Sit

down,

please!"

All through the land.

The feet on the bus go
Stomp, stomp, stomp!
Stomp, stomp, stomp!
Stomp, stomp, stomp!

The feet on the bus go

Stomp,

stomp, stomp!

All through
the land.

The raptors on the bus go

Pop, pop, pop!

Pop, pop, pop!

Pop, pop, pop!

The raptors on the bus go

Pop, pop, pop!

All through the land.

The bells on the bus go
Ding, ding, ding!
Ding, ding, ding!
Ding, ding, ding!

The bells on
the bus go

**Ding,
ding,
ding!**

All through
the land.

The grannies on the bus go,

"Shush,
shush,
shush!

Shush,
shush,
shush!

Shush,
shush,
shush!"

The dinos on the bus go up and down! Up and down! Up and down!

The dinos on the bus go **up** and **down**!

All through the land.

The dinos on the bus go,
"Eek, eek, eek!
Eek, eek, eek!
Eek, eek, eek!"

The dinos on the bus go,

"Eek,

The jaws behind the bus go
Open and shut!
Open and shut!
Open and shut!

The jaws behind the bus go

Open
and
shut!

All through the land.

The dinos on the bus go

Clap, clap, clap!

Clap, clap, clap!

Clap, clap, clap!

The dinos on the bus go

Clap, clap, clap!

All through the land.

The dinos on the bus go,
"Yawn, yawn, yawn!
Yawn, yawn, yawn!
Yawn, yawn, yawn!"

The dinos on the bus go,

"Yawn,

. . . All the way home!